For all my grandchildren
K.W.
For Louisa and Emma's grandparents
A.R.

Oxford University Press, Great Clarendon Street, Oxford OX2 6DP

Oxford   New York
Athens   Auckland   Bangkok   Bogota   Buenos Aires
Calcutta   Cape Town   Chennai   Dar es Salaam
Delhi   Florence   Hong Kong   Istanbul   Karachi
Kuala Lumpur   Madrid   Melbourne   Mexico City
Mumbai   Nairobi   Paris   São Paulo   Singapore
Taipei   Tokyo   Toronto   Warsaw

and associated companies in
Berlin   Ibadan

Oxford is a trade mark of Oxford University Press

Text copyright © Kathy Weston 1997
Illustrations copyright © Amelia Rosato 1997

First published 1997
Reprinted in paperback 1997, 1998

Kathy Weston and Amelia Rosato have asserted their moral
right to be known as the authors of the work.

A CIP catalogue record for this book is available
from the British Library

ISBN 0 19 279017 X (hardback)
ISBN 0 19 272337 5 (paperback)

Printed in Hong Kong

Granny
Goes to
Bethlehem

Kathy Weston
Illustrated by Amelia Rosato

Oxford University Press

Long, long ago, in a far-off land, a baby was
born in a stable.
    His mother's name was Mary . . .
but everyone knows this lovely story already.

What everyone doesn't know is that the
Three Wise Men and the Shepherds were
not the only visitors that night.

Rumbling along in their old
horse and cart came Mary's
mum and dad – Jesus's
granny and grandad.

And because they wouldn't
leave him behind, they had
brought their little dog,
Reuben, with them.

Reuben was a bit old and
a little bit smelly, but they
loved him anyway. They
had had him since Mary
was a little girl.

Now, Mary's mum didn't know *how* she'd known, but she'd just *known*. She supposed that something had told her to come.

As Mary's dad said, 'There was just no stopping her.'

'And just as well, if you ask me,' said Mary's mum, looking around her.

'Joseph! What were you thinking of – bringing our
Mary on such a journey just before the baby was due?
Good gracious! Is that a cow in here?
And who are all these old men? *And* a donkey!
Well I never!'

'Now, dear, calm down,' said Mary's dad.
'Come and see the baby. He's a lovely little chap.
Just like our Mary.'
    'Let's have a look at him, then,' she said.

'Ooh, Mary, what a little sweetheart!
He's certainly got your eyes.
Who's Granny's special boy, then?'

Meanwhile, Reuben had not taken to the Three Wise Men. Nor, indeed, had they taken to him. He had been yapping rather rudely at them since he arrived and was now tearing at the hem of the oldest one's cloak.

One of the Wise Men aimed a sly kick at Reuben. Jesus's granny saw this.

'Right!' she said, as she clapped her hands together. 'Thank you for coming and for all the lovely presents. But Mary needs her rest now and I'm sure you'll be wanting to be off.'

And the Three Wise Men rather agreed with her.

'Nothing very wise about the presents they brought you,'
Granny said, as she closed the door behind them.
'Grandad and I thought we'd give you a pram.'

'Joseph – I think that donkey and that cow would be better outside, don't you?' Granny said, in the sort of voice which really wasn't a question at all.

Joseph, who had been really quite relieved to see Granny, said, 'Okay, Granny, whatever you say.'

This made her smile in a pleased sort of way.

She bent over to tickle Jesus. 'Who's Granny's special boy, then?'

Jesus cooed and smiled at her.

'Look, Grandad,' said Granny, 'he's pleased to see us. And no wonder, with all these strangers about.'

'Now, Mary dear. About this lamb. It was very sweet of the Shepherds to bring him. But he'll grow into a sheep, you know, and where will you keep him then?

It'll be the story of the guinea-pigs all over again.'

'Best you take him back with you, dearies,' she said to the Shepherds as she showed them to the door.

Jesus gave a little whimper and Mary looked sad.

'You know, dear,' said Grandad, 'the lamb could share our old horse's stable, then Jesus could play with him when he comes to stay.'

'Oh, all right then, you old softy,' said his wife. 'But just you look after him.'

'We'll look after him together, won't we, Jesus?' said Grandad. He picked up baby Jesus who was now chuckling happily.

Granny sat down beside Mary. 'Well, our Mary. I will say that I was a bit upset. I wanted everything to be perfect for our first grandchild. But I must admit, this is *very* nice. Just the family.

Reuben! Will you leave that lamb alone! Funny. He doesn't usually like babies, but he does seem to have taken to our Jesus.'

'Aren't the stars wonderful tonight.
It's like they're shining just for Jesus.
  Oh, listen to me! What a silly old
Granny I am! 'Night, 'night, everyone.
'Night, 'night, Granny's special boy.'

'God bless!'